my first games readers ™

Chutes and Ladders™
Treasure Hunt

by Jackie Glassman
Illustrated by Suwin Chan

SCHOLASTIC INC.

New York   Toronto   London   Auckland   Sydney   Mexico City   New Delhi   Hong Kong   Buenos Aires

The  is shining.

The is blue.

Join our treasure hunt.

Let's find each clue.

Near the  ,

Past the ,

We race to find

Three gray .

Treasure Hunt

Next on the list

A buzzing .

I bet we can find one

By that apple .

Treasure Hunt

This one is easy!

A pretty pink .

We walk in the garden

And wiggle our !

Treasure Hunt

The  swing

Goes round and round.

A shiny

Is on the ground.

Treasure Hunt

Look what we found!

A  and .

And see inside,

There is a .

Treasure Hunt

Up in the

Almost out of sight,

A sailing blue diamond,

Hooray, it's a !

Treasure Hunt

It's time for lunch.

We like to share.

Inside one ,

We find a ![pear] !

Treasure Hunt

Off to the field

We go one and all,

To find the next clue,

A small, white ⚾.

Treasure Hunt

By the small ,

We each make a wish

Then throw in our coins.

Up jumps a !

Treasure Hunt

Under the

We take a short rest.

When we look up

We see a bird's .

Treasure Hunt

An ice cream

Is the very last thing.

We hear the

With its ding-a-ling ring.

Treasure Hunt

Did you spot all the picture clues in this Chutes & Ladders story poem?

Each picture clue is on a flash card. Ask a grown-up to cut out the flash cards. Then try reading the words on the back of the cards. The pictures will be your clue.

Have fun!

Sun	**Sky**
Swings	**Sandbox**
Rocks	**Fly**
Pie	**Rose**

Toes	Tire
Penny	Shovel
Pail	Snail
Kite	Bag

Pear	Baseball
Pond	Fish
Tree	Nest
Cone	Truck